Bear Feels Scared

Once upon a time, a writer felt scared. But standing by the writer's side was
a friend who gave the writer courage. The friend's name was Sarah Lanier
(who later became Sarah Goodrich). Dear friend, thank you. Write the novel.
With love – KW

For Sonia Chaghatzbanian
– JC

First published in Great Britain in 2008 by Simon & Schuster UK Ltd
Africa House, 64-78 Kingsway, London WC2B 6AH
A CBS COMPANY

Originally published in 2008 by Margaret K. McElderry Books,
an imprint of Simon & Schuster Children's Publishing Division, New York

Text copyright © 2008 Karma Wilson
Illustrations copyright © 2008 Jane Chapman
All rights reserved.

The rights of Karma Wilson and Jane Chapman to be identified as the author and illustrator of this work
have been asserted by them in accordance with the Copyright, Designs and Patents Act, 1988

All rights reserved including the right of reproduction in whole or in part in any form.

A CIP catalogue record for this book is available from the British Library upon request.

ISBN: 978 1 84738 250 4 (PB)

Printed in Italy

1 3 5 7 9 10 8 6 4 2

Bear Feels Scared

Karma Wilson

illustrations by Jane Chapman

SIMON AND SCHUSTER

London   New York   Sydney   Toronto

*I*n the deep, dark woods
by the Strawberry Vale,
a big bear lumbers
down a small, crooked trail.

Bear's tummy growls
as he looks for a snack.
But it's cold, cold, cold,
so the bear turns back.

He is not home yet when the sun starts to set . . .

And the bear feels scared . . .

Bear shakes and he shivers
as a storm starts to howl.
Bear mutters, "What is that?
Are there spooks on the prowl?"

The path gets dimmer
and the sky grows grey.
Bear looks to and fro,
but he can't find his way.

He huddles by a tree and he wails,
"Poor me!"

And the bear
feels
scared . . .

Meanwhile, back
in the warm, cosy lair,
friends start to worry
for their poor, lost Bear.

"It is late," Mouse squeaks,
"and our Bear doesn't roam."
"There's a storm!" cries Hare.
"Shouldn't Bear be home?"

Wren tweets from his perch, "We must all go and search!

What if Bear feels scared?"

The friends bundle up
and begin to prepare.
They form a search party
for their lost friend Bear.

But Bear is all alone
and he sheds big tears.
There's a noise in the forest
and he feels big fears.

Bear trembles in the wind. How he longs for a friend.

And the bear

feels

scared . . .

Badger lights a lamp
and he shouts, "Let's go!
All the birds search high
while the rest search low."

With a flounce and a flutter
they set off together.
They trudge down the trail
through the wild, wet weather.

They call, "Hey, Bear, are you there? Are you there?"

And the bear feels scared.

But he perks up his ears.
Is it Mole calling out?
And is that Hare's voice?
Does Bear hear him shout?

Wren, Owl, and Raven
all squawk from the sky,
"It is Bear! He is there!"
And they sigh big sighs.

By a tree waits Bear, ten feet from his lair!

And the bear
looks
scared.

With a flap and flurry
all the friends gather near.
They give him bear hugs –
they calm his bear fears.

Later in the night,
all clustered in a heap,
the bear tells stories
while his friends fall asleep.

Cuddled up tight, they snore through the night.

And the bear

feels

safe.